JACKIE and the SHADOW SNATCHER

JACKIE and the SHADOW SNATCHER

by LARRY DI FIORI

ALFRED A. KNOPF   NEW YORK

FOR MY SON, LARSON

THIS IS A BORZOI BOOK PUBLISHED BY ALFRED A. KNOPF

Published in the United States by Alfred A. Knopf, an imprint of Random House Children's Books, a division of Random House, Inc., New York.

KNOPF, BORZOI BOOKS, and the colophon are registered trademarks of Random House, Inc.

www.randomhouse.com/kids

Educators and librarians, for a variety of teaching tools, visit us at www.randomhouse.com/teachers

Library of Congress Cataloging-in-Publication Data
Di Fiori, Lawrence.
Jackie and the Shadow Snatcher / Lawrence Di Fiori. — 1st ed.
p.   cm.
SUMMARY: To retrieve his lost shadow, a brave little boy makes his way to the hideout of an infamous criminal.
ISBN 0-375-87515-8 (trade) — ISBN 0-375-97515-2 (lib. bdg.)
[1. Shadows—Fiction. 2. Lost and found possessions—Fiction.] I. Title.
PZ7.D542Jac 2006 [E]—dc22
2005018290

MANUFACTURED IN CHINA
10 9 8 7 6 5 4 3 2 1
First Edition

BEHIND MY HOUSE, DOWN BY THE RIVER, IS A BOAT. USE IT TO CROSS OVER TO THE SHADOW SNATCHER'S HIDEOUT.

EH, W-WHAT SHOULD I SAY TO HIM?

YOU'LL THINK OF SOMETHING. JUST BE BRAVE. AND GET BACK WHAT BELONGS TO YOU.

SURE, SURE... GULP!

SHADOW SNATCHER! WHY DON'T THEY TELL US ABOUT THIS SORT OF STUFF IN SCHOOL?

AW, RATS! IT'S GOING TO BE A LOT OF WORK TO ROW ACROSS THIS RIVER.

TO THE BOAT, BAXTER!

JEEPERS! BAXTER, IT'S GETTING LATE...

...IF WE HURRY, I BET WE CAN STILL GET HOME BEFORE MOM.